by Lynn Hodges and Sue Buchanan   illustrated by John Bendall-Brunello

Angels Watching Over Me

ZONDERkidz

ZONDERVAN.com/
AUTHORTRACKER
follow your favorite authors

ZONDERKIDZ

Angels Watching Over Me
Copyright © 2005 by Lynn Hodges and Sue Buchanan
Illustrations © 2005 by John Bendall-Brunello

This title is also available as a Zondervan ebook.
Visit www.zondervan.com/ebooks.

Requests for information should be addressed to:

Zonderkidz, Grand Rapids, Michigan 49530

ISBN 978-0-310-72816-0

Editor: Amy De Vries
Cover design: Cindy Davis

Printed in China

12 13 14 15 16 17 /LPC/ 10 9 8 7 6 5 4 3 2 1

*The Lord will command his angels
to take good care of you.*
Psalm 91:11

On the day that God made you the angels stood by,
They giggled and kissed you and then gave a sigh:

Oh, how can we help you? What can we do
To keep this child safe and trusting in you?

God told them his plan on that special day—
They would watch you and keep you at work
and at play.

God, thank you for angels that watch over me,
For keeping me safe from the things I can't see.
For all of my lifetime, I'll rest with this thought—
There are angels around me. God loves me a lot!

What is an angel and what are they for?
I know that they guard me: I wish I knew more.

Do they laugh when I laugh?
Do they cry when I'm sad?

Do they sleep when I sleep?
Do they smile when I'm glad?

What is an angel?

Are they **big**?

Are they small?

Do they jump cloud to cloud?

Do they come when I call?

I think they play harps—

And at Christmas, they sing.

God, thank you for angels that watch over me,
For keeping me safe from the things I can't see.
For all of my lifetime, I'll rest with this thought—
There are angels around me. God loves me a lot!

What is an angel? Are they here day and night?
Do they cheer, do they clap, when I do what is right?

When I'm thinking of saying what should not be said,
Do they hear the same "shush" that I hear in my head?

God, thank you for angels that watch over me,
For keeping me safe from the things I can't see.
For all of my lifetime, I'll rest with this thought—
There are angels around me. God loves me a lot!

What is an angel?

Do they twirl?

Do they dance?

Do they keep me from danger—

From taking a chance?

When I'm thinking of going where I shouldn't go
Do they cartwheel on rainbows, when I wisely choose "no."

God, thank you for angels that watch over me,
For keeping me safe from the things I can't see.
For all of my lifetime, I'll rest with this thought—
There are angels around me. God loves me a lot!

There are angels around us.
God loves us a lot!